The Serpent
And the forbidden
fruit

The serpent and the forbidden fruit

And other short stories

Copyright Henrik Neergaard 2020

Published by: Books-on-Demand,
Copenhagen, Denmark

Printed by: Books-on-Demand, Norderstedt,
Germany

ISBN: 9788743026198

Henrik Neergaard

The serpent and
The forbidden fruit

And other short stories

Books-on-Demand

Do not let the sun go down over your anger

Uncle Richard was a firm believer in the good old adage that "one should not la the sun go down over his wrath", and therefore every night (or at least at least every other) Aunt Olga gave a proper dung to get rid of his anger before he lay down to sleep. Almost every night, Aunt Olga also had a whole host of things about him that annoyed her violently – not so much because she was particularly violent or hot, but probably more so because Uncle Richard could be quite annoying in many respects, although he usually strives throughout the day to keep calm and not let his temper run away. , and even often also tried to think directly positively about the things that once happened.

But during the evening, it sizzled and bubbled in him with pent-up outrage and the like, which he then had to release anyway before bed, so he got rid of all the accumulated anger of the day before the night fell on.

Aunt Olga, for her part, she felt violated by all the unreasonable accusations that he let hail at her night after night, and then had no children (at least no one who was still at home) that she could have scolded for lack of better, she instead went in to the neighbor's wife and repeated the usual svada about How badly they cut the hedge, failed to prune the trees and did not clear proper snow in winter and what might otherwise be of the kind of grievance.

This became the neighbour's wife so angry that she woke up her husband, who used to go to bed early, so she could give him a proper dung so she too could avoid letting the sun go down over her anger.

Her husband in turn – he probably reacted in a slightly atypical way. Now he also got a solid amount of anger that he needed to get rid of, so he also didn't let the sun go down over his anger. So he got out of bed and took his notepad and set out to write the most demeaning and sarcastic remarks he could make about his wife and her completely misplaced and unjustified scolding, which she had even awakened him from his early evening slums to shed on him.

He carefully wrote his formulations through several times, and each time they were honed more and more until they were sharp and at the same time amusing, so that they could – at least in his own opinion – be used in a revue text or by a stand-but-comedian who skin-braided his utterly unreasonable wife, in a way that so that the whole hall of the imaginary audience lay flat with laughter and rewarded him with a roaring applause. It usually took an hour or an hour or a half for him to get this far, and in the meantime his wife had long since gone to bed in her bedroom up on the first floor and was sleeping her sweet sleep.

Then he sneaked into the living room, where that big ugly potted plant stood, which was a gift from his not very much-loved mother-in-law, and which he had always hated with a good heart. After closing various doors behind him so he was sure not to wake up the wife, he stood up in front of the big ugly potted plant with today's manuscript in hand and began to recite his text with all its witty points and well-turned, sarcastic formulations for mother-in-law's potted plant, as if the poor potted plant, which fortunately did not understand a damn of What was going on was an audience at a performance with him as the famous and cheery stand-up comedian who every night drew full houses to his performances.

Co-writer's annotation:

As the co-writer of these texts, there are two comments that need to be made so that readers do not have to wonder too much about why this strange little text has, however, been included in this selection of thoroughly serious and deeply thought-provoking pieces of text.

Comment No. 1 (The Social Realism): I wonder if the author of this text has really thought about how residents far north of the

Arctic Circle are handling it there by not letting the sun go down over its wrath? Those who live so high to the north that there are months of winter darkness and correspondingly several months when the sun does not go down at all? So perhaps his text is not as universal as he may think.

Comment No. 2 (The Creative): there is an important addition that the author of this text has completely forgotten to include. This is mainly about the husband of the neighbour. I have heard persistent rumours that, like any sensible entrepreneur, he has used this daily challenge as a starting point for a business idea that is well on his way to making him a really wealthy man with a large and successful company. It started with her mother-in-law's ugly pot plant starting to ailing, so the wife took it up the windowsill of her bedroom so she could care for and care for it. Then he couldn't use it as an audience anymore. And there weren't any of the other potted plants he would expose to that sort of thing. So he made a slightly primitive sculpture that was supposed to envision mother-in-law's potted plant. But now he wanted to move on. Why not make a sculpture of a person – or at least a person's head – instead. He was probably a bit of a wit, so he didn't dare make someone who was supposed to imagine neither the wife nor the mother-in-law. So instead, he made one to imagine a well-known politician from a party he didn't like.

Soon after, he read about those Japanese tamagotchis. And about other kinds of robots and artificial pets. Now it was not a pet he wanted to create, but a creature you could scold, so that you could react to your anger, and who, mind you, reacted to what it was scolded for by looking sad, or saying sorry and being embarrassed by what it was criticised for.

And in fact, with the help of some skilled technicians and partners, he managed within a few years to create a whole range of such scolding robots that you could react to all the disappointments and frustrations and aggressions of the day – at least verbally – so that you did not let the sun go down over your anger.

And it became the basis of the great international company he has built. So it's his contribution to doing something good for the world while earning a lot of millions for himself. And just think, this important point, the author of the above paragraph had completely forgotten to include. And I had otherwise made completely different plans for what I was going to do.

Comment No. 3: Of course, I know that what is usually meant by not letting the sun go down over its anger usually means something about sat down and forgive everything between heaven and earth, or something like that. But then no story would have come out of it, would it?

And if the neighbor's wife in the tale had done that, then her husband would never have made up that invention and create that great company and become a rich and esteemed man who has even done something for the benefit of others, well!

The serpent and the forbidden fruit

That's one of Harold's stories. The guy I'd
met who had told me about my father. He'd
been in some of that socialist thing with my
dad. He sent me a few other old flyers from
that time. They look pretty old-fashioned.
One of them is one that he has written
himself. They were certainly in politics at the
time. With all those little homemade printed
matter that they shared out all sorts of
places. That was before the internet, so that

was obviously the way to do it back then. This one he sent me was actually a little funny. It was such a rather alternative version of the story of Adam and Eve and the fall of sin back then in the Garden of Eden. He just gave it a completely different twist, so it fit into his political views. He's changed a lot of the point, so it came to suit his other agitation. Here comes the text from it:

Our Lord had repeatedly warned Adam and Eve not to eat of the forbidden fruit. That is, the great juicy apples that grew on the Tree of Knowledge. For many years, Adam and Eve had bonded with themselves and resisted this temptation, for they were both obedient and responsible and had no intention of doing anything that they were not allowed to do.

Eva and Adam were standing near the tree, a day when the October sun made the apples look even more beautiful and more tempting

than otherwise. But they were determined to
still comply with the ban on eating from
them. They were in the process of picking
some of the juicy fruits on the small shrubs
and barely anxious the apples on the Tree of
Knowledge.

But suddenly Eva spotted a snake
meandering through the grass while hissing
scarily. It played up the yawn so that the
gapy tongue played in the air. It was
heading straight for Adam, but I don't think
he'd noticed it yet. From the entire
appearance of the snake, it looked like it
would chop when it reached Adam, which
was only a few feet away.

Eva shouted a warning to Adam, but she
knew that a human couldn't run from a
snake. Of course, she wanted to protect her
beloved Adam from being bitten by the
snake. But all she could do was quickly pluck
a really big and low-hanging apple from the
Tree of Knowledge, which she stood right

next to, and rush to throw it at the snake of all force, hoping to smash the head of the snake, or at least divert the snake's attention from Adam.

It failed to crush the snake's head, because it takes more than a big apple. But she managed to deflect its attention from Adam. The snake usually ate mostly mice and rats and bird cubs, but it hadn't eaten anything for weeks, so it was ravenously hungry. Therefore, it greedily threw itself at the big juicy apple that had ended up in the grass right in front of it. By the time it had finished swallowing the apple, it had become drowsy by the big meal, and rolled itself up and put themselves to sleep, as snakes have a habit of eating when they have eaten themselves sated. Therefore, Adam and eve also avoided being attacked and bitten by the snake. They praised their luck and Eva's quickness and rushed to another place in the garden, away from where the snake had gone to sleep while it digested his meal.

But the accident was that the apple it had eaten was from the Tree of Knowledge. Now it had all the knowledge and wisdom that existed in the world, and thus it had become much wiser than both Eve and Adam. And since it was once a snake, all its knowledge of good and evil was most in the strange evil and cunning intrigue. Therefore, the snake managed to fool Adam and Eve quite quickly and told them that it was their job to feed it and its entire large family. So now Adam and Eve had to wear it and work almost 24 hours a day to catch mice and small birds and collect eggs and cubs from the nests of birds to feed all the greedy snakes. Although they didn't like it and thought it was disgusting, they had been tricked by the cunning snake into thinking they had to do it anyway.

Our Lord and his park officials soon discovered, of course, that an apple had been picked from the Tree of Knowledge and that the ban had thus been violated. One of the park rangers had even seen Eva pluck the apple from one of the lower branches on the tree, but then he had turned around because one of the others was calling him and hadn't seen the rest of what was happening. He immediately reported what he had seen to our Lord, who summoned Eve and Adam for an interview and rebuked them, because they had been dealing so recklessly with the apples of the forbidden tree and was to blame for the fact that the secret and forbidden knowledge had now ended up with the wretched and nequering creep. As punishment, both Adam and Eve and the snake were banished from the Garden of Eden.

But once they had entered the much more harsh and hard world outside, the cunning snake could even better use his knowledge and cunningness to exploit Adam and Eve. And that is the explanation for the fact that Eve and Adam and all their descendants have ever since had to spend most of their

time working on the hard work of the sweat
of their faces to obtain food and other goods
for all the snakes and all the other cunning
creepers and parasites that have therefore
been able to eat large and fat and collect all
the riches of the world.

Co-writer's annotation:

This is, after all, a completely unauthorized
interpretation of the ancient and very
central narrative. Sometimes I do not quite
know what is going on with the author. But
according to my contract with the first layer,
I am probably going to have to incorporate
it in the collection anyway.

Hard work should always give a pay-off

Once upon a time, there were three brothers. Actually, it wasn't very long ago, so they're probably here yet. The three brothers inherited 5 million, 2 million and half million from an old aunt, respectively. Your rich uncle, uncle, multimillionaire, is multimillionaire and childless. He is obsessed with the idea that it should pay off to work — he has worked himself out of nowhere and built up a large and rich company through hard work — he despises the sons of fathers who have inherited the foundation of their wealth and then just live a life of idleness The three brother sons are the closest heirs to his great company and fortune – he will test them and see , which of them is most suitable to take over and continue his large group.

The eldest son gets $5 million in test money - he gets an idea for an app for a smart phone and puts a group of technicians to put the idea into practice and hires people for all the tasks to develop it - it quickly makes a big return, and he moves to a giant luxury villa in Hawaii, where he enjoys a luxury life while the money from the app is just ticking into the account.

The middle son gets 2 million – he invests the money in shares to increase them – at first it goes well, but then he misjudges some shares that suddenly plummet in value – there are other failed investments, so he loses the money and becomes poor, but has in the meantime married a wife who has a permanent job as a schoolteacher and who is supporting him , so he can only cultivate his keen interest in angling in the nearby lake, because he does not really bother to do a regular job.

Youngest brother is angry that he has received so much less than the other two – it is too little to invest or start a business for, he believes – and his father-in-law is trying to get the money out of him so he can pay off his constant gambling debts. So youngest son goes drinking with all the money on him --- but he gets scared to meet his father-in-law in a tavern and that he should then coax the money out of him --- so he puts it in a box and digs them into a park he randomly comes by, behind some bushes.

It happened a Friday night before he goes out into town on a drinking spree with a few thousand dollars on him ----- but afterwards he can't remember where it was, he dug the money down --- but then they are safe for the greedy father-in-law ---- he takes work cleaning, drives taxi, and works hard in such jobs so he can save together to buy himself a decent home.

After two years, the tests will be decided.

The rich uncle rejects the eldest brother, even though he has made the 5 million to turn into 150 mill, for he has had others do all the work, and the finished app just runs by itself like a money machine – a la Mister 10 percent for brokering the purchase of food, or concert tickets etc. – what the uncle calls to parasitic the work of others

He also rejects the middle brother who has lost all the 2 million. On failed stock trades.

So he wills his entire fortune to the youngest son who comes to the family meeting in his dirty work clothes and downcastly admits that he can't find the place where he dug the money down, but they had to lie in a safe place precisely because he didn't find them ---and therefore neither has been able to use them el has been able to give them to his charlatan by a father-in-law That claims he has a great idea to invest them so they make a fantastic return --- instead, youngest son has worked hard all the time, while brother 1 lives in luxury in Hawaii and just lets the money flow into the account, and brother 2 has invested wildly with the money and lost it and otherwise just relaxed in idleness and found a wife that support him, even if she just has a regular job as a schoolteacher.

Co-writer's annotation:

Here, too, the author has embarked on a solid and thorough reinterpretation of an ancient myth that everyone else agrees on how to be perceived. He gives it a completely different meaning, almost so that it will be about the same thing as what is called the Matthew effect. It is, after all, the one with that "he who has a great deal already will be given more, but he who has nothing from him shall even be taken as he has," as my great-grandmother's old Bible stated.

The mystery of the ancient Marbles in The King's Garden

This is something one of my friends told me. In the city of Copenhagen, there is park called The King's Garden. Today it is a public park, but once it was only for the king and the royal family. There is even a castle, dating back to the 17th century. In the park, there are some very marble balls. I think the diameter of each one is at least one meter, maybe a little bit more. They are just lying around there in the park. I guess nobody really knows what they have been used for.

The story that I have told, goes as this:

A slightly mysterious man from the alternative treatment environment uses them as a kind of fortune-teller. That's what he calls it. Among others, to an eccentric and rich old lady, who is of course either an old maiden or a widowed lady in whom he has beaten the claws. a kind of home-knitted and maybe slightly acidic version of I Ching, or similar. At least he uses that comparison himself.

He has had a ring made of wood that can be laid down around the top of the large marbles. In the tree ring there are 15 small recesses, each with a number painted next to it. Then he puts a little bullet, for example. A billiard ball or a ping pong ball perched on top of the large marble and he gives it a small gentle push so that it trundles down and lands in one of the 15 recesses of that ring of wood he has first put down around the marble. And then he has written down some cryptic phrasings, kind of horoscope-like, that it will happen or that, or she should pay special attention to this or that.

It has to be convincing, so he has written the text on some large sheets of paper that look old and mysterious, with headlines with intricate Gothic letters, old copper plugs about alchemy, occult symbols, etc.

And the text he has gradually worked out in more detail, so that these are some long very cryptic formulations that can be interpreted or interpreted in many different ways, so that it will appear as an occult message to his client – which for the time being is mostly the rich old lady.

For each of the large marbles in the King's Garden there is a certain aspect, he claims. One of them is about the prehistory of the problem, another about the present – about the future – about relationships – about proper way of life – obstacles – health – travel and experiences – resources to draw on – economics – the core of a problem – and finally one that gives concrete directions of action – for example, the need to understand the future of the problem.

For example, a particular investment – establishing a contact or invitation to a specific person – an important symbolic act – reading a particular book - seeking out a particular place – major purchases and new acquisitions – traveling, etc. He has also produced some large, beautiful sheets of paper on each of these, with the same kind of cryptic formulations that he can interpret and interpret over again almost as he pleases – in the style of, for example, the following: a tarot attache.

In fact, it is the lady's nephew – or son/daughter, that it is a little unclear to me

– who has turned to the imaginative alternative therapist because he is concerned that the lady is in the process of desolating her and thus the family's riches away on dubious investments etc. – perhaps she lives on a large old manor house, which is decaying and where the operation is being neglected, so that it causes more and more deficits.

The nephew has tried to speak her mind, but has not come to her senses. Incidentally, he also has a name, the one who alternative treats, he is called something quite ordinary like Hans Nielsen.

But he doesn't know that his nephew really has a hidden agenda of getting his aunt to behave financially in certain ways, such as investing in a company that he's about to start with a few of his friends.

But of course it won't be long before the nephew and the alternative therapist come together to take joint advantage of the old lady. At the same time, of course, they're also trying to cheat each other. And then it might turn out that the old lady is much more cunning than they think, so it ends up with her taking the out of both of the other two who are trying so hard to cheat on her.

Co-writer's annotation:

Yes, there could almost be a crime novel. Or a nice Danish film, admittedly a little older, with some of the atmosphere from the Olsen Gang films. But that's probably the time from now on. So perhaps that is why the author has not bothered to write on it, but has thrown himself into other tasks in which there is hopefully a little more perspective.

But it's up to the authors and all the other actors in these media industries. I'm just a small hard-working fee slave trying to make me a way of taking on the work as a co-writer of a collection of highly mixed sweets like this. Because I actually often think that the author of this one gets around it, but it's possible that readers think it's very good anyway. That would actually be the best thing. Not least from the fore subject's eyes.

A story of three genera- tions

This is just a little thing to think about for a moment.

3 teenagers have a rich ancient aunt who gives the poor family members – especially the young – clothes, gadgets, etc. She has also done so with their mother and their grandmother earlier on. She is very old now, in her nineties, probably.

Grandma wrote letters about her wishes —
the aunt could only read the words and
couldn't reveal if it was real need —
something they really needed, or just greed
for getting as much as possible --- so she was
guided by what and how much they wrote
about how grateful they were for it — and
how much they praised her and pleased her.

At the next generation, they had been on the
phone — and now their mother called her
aunt and asked for what she needed. Now
Auntie could hear her voice and her way of
speaking, whether it was a sincere wish or
just something she wanted to do.

In our time — with the three young teenagers
— you have moved on to communicating with
text messages or other text messages — e.g.
Facebook, so now Auntie has to rely again
on the words they write, and it is once again
the expressed gratitude and the goofiness
that will be the decisive factor.

She lived out on East Paradise Boulevard

I once knew a woman who lived on East Paradise Boulevard. She was feeling very bad. Very unhappy. Later she moved on to West Paradise Boulevard, and she got much better, much happier. And she got married.

Ten years later, I met her again. And now, she was even more unhappy than before.

But then she moved back to a house on East Paradise Boulevard, albeit a different one from the one she first lived in, and it was clear to see that she was feeling much better. At least, she got a divorce from her husband.

Just a little bit about

chaos and

cosmos -

and an unexpected synthesis

Most people know there's chaos and then there's the cosmos. Or should I mention them in the opposite order, to emphasize that it is the cosmos I keep with? In any case, you usually reckon it was chaos that

came first. Of the two concepts, that is. And
then eventually came the cosmos. It was
then split in two over time, i.e. in a
conceptual way. Microcosm and macrocosm.
So – one is a thesis about macrocosm, which
is the world we see around us, and then
someone came up with an antithesis called
microcosm, and is what goes on inside our
heads and those kinds of places.

But now it is also quite well known that man
does not live on bread alone, nor on wine
alone. At least not if you are a nice and
sensible citizen. Not even of altern's wine,
unless you are a big culprit with much to be
forgiven for, and then you are not a nice and
sensible citizen either. Not from the general
view, at least.

But that's why nature has been so wise and
clever and everything, so it has come up with
something. It may have also read something
of one of those old German philosophers
named Hegel. At least that's about thesis -

antithesis - synthesis as it's called. But nature thought it had to be a little on the way to humans, when they themselves had such a hard time figuring it out.

So it gave us a lot of time and free (I think I think, but I'm also often an optimist) a synthesis for those two opposites called microcosm and macrocosm. And that synthesis is, of course, called the abri-cosmos – or, as some prefer to pronounce it, abrocos-moss.

But I just want to remind you that if you eat too much of that abri-cosmos (or apricot moss), you risk getting a little chaos in your stomach – and starting it all over again. First there was chaos, and then, through some effort on our part (or just by letting time pass) there is a calm and pleasant cosmos out of chaos. That's how the world is so wisely decorated, it's said.

Co-writer's annotation:

Here again, there is something that the author has forgotten to explain properly. Two things, actually.

Omission No. 1: The author of this post seems to assume that all people automatically prefer the cosmos to chaos. But this is by no means the case. In fact, few people have got a taste for seasoning their cosmos with greater or lesser amounts of chaos. Almost like those who become dilapidated to ever more powerful forms of chili, for example. Like everything else, of course, it can also take the upper hand.

But perhaps the most strange thing is that the biggest and most violent ness of chaos is very often disguised as something to restore some kind of cosmos that the people claim have been lost. And it can be confusing to many people, and has, from experience, often done so.

Omission No. 2: The author also forgets to mention completely that, in addition to apricot moss and microcosm and macrocosm, there is actually a fourth variant of this cosmos concept. And it's even extremely easy to find. Simply omit the first two letters of the word macrocosm. Then you discover the extremely interesting but very overlooked concept called chromosco. Or to underline the point, the chromo-cosmos. Many will probably argue that it could also be a bid for some kind of synthesis between chaos and the cosmos, at least in fairly well-run, yet not entirely boring taverns, when it is not going on at all.

A very nice Cup of Tea indeed it is

The weather had changed. It was sunny
weather again. Clear blue sky with beautiful
white clouds, and actually quite warm.
Moster Marna liked that. Maybe they could
sit out in the garden for their morning tea.
They drank morning tea every day of the
year. Exactly half eleven. It was one of their
fixed traditions, which they kept in
contention, year after year. They took turns,
every other day she was the one who boiled
water on the big old-fashioned stove and
brewed the tea and greased the french bread

sandwiches that belonged, and every other day it was Uncle Ola who was in charge of it.

Ola actually was born in Norway, but he had lived in this country since he was 18. Back then, almost many years ago, his parents had moved here because his mother had got a job as an engineer at a big shipyard, called Burmeister and Wain, who at the time still existed and were one of the major companies in the iron industry. It wasn't that common back then. I mean, a woman was an engineer, even in a big shipyard.

By the way, it wasn't ships she was working on to construct. It was something much more exciting. I think it's safe to say that. Burmeister and Wain did things other than ships. For example, they had a large engine factory where they built diesel engines for ships. But that's not where she worked, either. Not until later, at least. It was in a smaller department that involved building airplanes. Even before airplanes became commonplace. In the childhood of the flight, you might say. But it only turned into some prototypes that weren't put into production anyway when it came down to it. Which she thought was a completely wrong decision.

His father, on the other hand, was a upholsterer, and you could be almost anywhere. At least back then, when people weren't nearly as infected with use and throw away the mindset as most became today. Back then, it was more common to protect the things you had, rather than constantly replacing them with something new and smarter. Solid quality items, such as old heirlooms that might have been passed down in a family for generations, were much more appreciated.

In fact, it turned out that the market for upholstery and general refurbishment of older solid quality furniture was somewhat larger in this country. Or possibly it was because they had settled in an affluent neighborhood where there was quite a lot of that kind of furniture. Or maybe it could also be because people down here didn't take quite such a good look at their stuff, so they got worn out faster and needed reholstery. But anyway, he quickly built a thriving business as a furniture upholsterer. A good and solidly based small company with a dozen employees.

Then, when Ola had finished 24, he married Marna, who came from a customs family in a larger provincial town somewhere in Jutland. There is no question in saying anything else about the location of the city. In fact, it's a little unfair to call it a customs family. Because only her father was a customs officer. Her mother was a fairly ordinary housewife, a term many still used back then. She took care of house and home and children and cooking and cleaning and gardening and big washing and blob washing and wasting and washing up and dog and cat and everything else that just belonged to such a household back then.

At the time, it was not very strenuous to be a customs official, especially if you had a slightly senior position and sat in an office. Therefore, they had time to drink morning tea every day at the customs office where he was employed. Exactly at half eleven, with lunch not to be held. At the time, of course, it was not the customs officials themselves who prepared their morning tea. You had people like that, as was said at the time.

"People" was in this case the old Miss Petersen, who had been employed at the customs office for a lifetime and who therefore probably knew how to plan a proper morning tea, prepare, prepare, prepare and serve. As well as consumed in a noble and cultured way. No, not just consumed, but enjoyed. Coffee was something you drank, but it had to be enjoyed. That was Ms. Petersen's attitude to it, and she didn't deviate from it.

When her father, old Herr Petersen, who was also Aunt Marna's father, finally retired from the customs office, he took home the tradition of drinking morning tea every morning at just half eleven. However, he still did not cook the morning tea. It was not Miss Petersen either, but her sister, who was married to old Herr Petersen and was named Aunt Marna's mother. We always called her that. He calmly put his faithful wife and wife to that every day of the year.

As Aunt Marna herself grew and began to become more aware of how things were intertwined, both at home and in society and in some other places, she was greatly outraged by this one-sided distribution of tasks, and wondered in particular that her mother easily put up with it. And so it was. But she had to wait many years before it got serious.

And yet the tradition of the morning tea had become so ingrained with her too, so she took it with her into her marriage. However, with some changes. As long as she and her husband - who was Uncle Ola - went to work, it was only Saturday and Sunday that they could drink morning tea together, and then it didn't happen to them. Only when they had both retired could it really happen, as they called it then.

Now they started drinking morning tea every day. Every day. Exactly half eleven, just like in his time at the customs office in the small town at the other end of the country. But she had insisted from the outset on a fairer division of labour. Every second it was herself who was in charge of preparing their morning tea, and every day it was her husband Ola. To her great amazement (but, of course, also joy), Ola had not objected to this at all.

In reality, he almost enjoyed standing there in the kitchen, boiling water and brewing it and smearing french bread with cheese and strawberry jam and orange jam. Funnily enough, he was actually the one who was most eager to maintain exactly the way it had been done at the longest-abandoned customs office, and it was all the way down to the smallest detail. After all, he had only heard of how it was going on at the time and had never, I believe, ever set foot in a customs office.

But perhaps that was precisely why he had had such a nostalgic relationship with it, because that is exactly what he had. Based on the many stories he had heard of it, he had come to perceive it as the very symbol of good old-fashioned cozy coziness from the time before the world went low. After he had retired and had therefore come up in the years and had started to care more about this kind of thing.

He was starting to really care about the very small details. For example, he stubbornly insisted that it should be exactly the same kind of the, the very same variety that he called that had been used at the time at the customs office. Although it could eventually be difficult to obtain and had to be purchased in a specialty store in a remote neighbouring town. At least pretty remote of a neighboring town to be.

There was a real trade in a small side street. It was a really exclusive and, by the way, incredibly cozy specialty shop, which was kept entirely in the old style and where they sold several hundred different kinds of tea. And only the, or accessories for the brewing, the last, however, only to a limited extent. And where, by the way, there was an incredibly sweet and smiling female clerk who made an incredible effort to hold on to the most rewarding and most regular customers, to which Ola eventually heard.

So she always took care very lovingly and accommodating of his need for just the special kind of tea, even though it had to be picked up from a shelf high up where she had to climb onto a ladder that he had to keep for her.

By contrast, Aunt Marna liked to experiment a little more. Whatever the case, she had also discovered the very same exclusive thehandel in the remote neighbouring town, but apparently independent of Ola. So every two months she was the one who took the car and drove to the old cozy thehandel in the neighboring town to buy it for their regular morning ritual, which it had gradually evolved into.

She was thrilled with all the many choices that were available. As I said, several hundred different thesorts in stock in the exclusive thehandel, so there was enough to get started on.

Walking around the shop alone was quite an experience for her. She enjoyed exploring all the many exciting and almost always extremely fragrant and aromatic the varieties that often originated from otherwise little-known thedistricties far from the beaten track. Fortunately, there was an immensely friendly and very welcoming male clerk who, with almost infinite patience, climbed the ladder and picked the various thesorts down from even the highest shelves for her, only for her to enjoy their aroma and have perhaps a dozen – or a whole dozen, for that matter – to choose from when she had to make the hard choice about which one it should be this time.

On the contrary, she showed great thoroughness and serious and considered care and appointed the one she liked the one she liked best on this special day, which, it seems, should be a new one that she had not tried before. Then she told him which one she wanted. In doing so, he made himself to weigh the desired quantity, because this too was done at the same time in the good, old-fashioned and completely traditional way.

Of course, it could often be difficult to remember exactly which of the many different kinds of tea she had tried before, but here too the nice clerk came to her aid. He had a small notebook with her name beautifully calligraphed on the outside. He then took it out after each of her purchases, carefully listing which variety she had bought this time. The next time she came to the store, he could then wonder if the one she then considered buying was already listed in the little notebook, so that she could avoid the kind of boring mistakes that she might later regret.

It turned out that it was a service he provided to a large number of regular customers who kept coming into the store year after year. However, this only disappointed her for a very short time before she realised that there was no reason to do so when he was providing such an excellent service as he did, and which could be quite difficult, not to say almost impossible, to drive up many other places today.

So she was happy with her visits to the trade. She was always happy and uplifted, and felt almost rejuvenated when, later in the day or out of the evening, she came home from her visits to the wonderful tea shop.

All of this is actually told just to illustrate the difference between Olas and her widely differing approach to the purchases. And so it was only at that point that their habits differed. When it came to the brewing and the preservation in the home itself, there were no significant differences. They both stuck to the overall framework for when and how their daily morning tea was to take place.

French bread was to be served, and it should be poppy French bread. It was fixed. The good poppy french bread from the right artisan baker. Neither sieve bread, sour bread, graham bread nor some of the various modern forms of coarse core bread. It was all fixed for both. Not that they were fanatics. not at all. The coarse bread and the sunflower seeds and 3-grain bread and 5-grain bread and spelt bread and chia bread, and whatever else you thought of putting in the bread these days, could be good enough for other occasions.

But not for their morning tea. There it should be french bread with birches. Nothing else could be said. And it was not to be the blue birches, because it was not used for French bread at the time at the customs office, of which they had heard so many reports. And certainly not at the bakery where the French bread for the customs office's morning tea was always purchased by the stoute and diligent Miss Petersen every morning at five minutes past ten minutes. Of course, they should have fresh french bread every day. Day-old bread would not fit at all for customs office staff, that would be an almost unthinkable thought.

What was going on the bread was also completely fixed. First, a generous layer of butter. Not margarine, not even plant marggarine. Nor did any of the mixed products that are gradually coming onto the market. Really good, old-fashioned butter. They had had a little dispute over whether the butter should be organic or not. Uncle Ola was against it. Not because he was against ecology as such. It just didn't belong in this context, he said. The crux of his argument was that it would be wrong to buy organic butter for the purpose, since such a product was not marketed at the time many years ago, when Marna's father was a customs officer, and that it would therefore be a break with tradition.

Conversely, Marna claimed that at that time – and it was many years ago – all agricultural products were basically organic, without knowing it, so to speak, because that was before you started using chemical fertilisers and chemical sprays and all that sort of thing. And that's why, she thought, it would be just the best way to uphold the tradition if they made sure to buy butter that was clearly labeled as organic. Because then it was just sure that it was the same good old kind of butter as then. After all, it was the content, that is, the butter, that should correspond to tradition, she said, and not what was left on the packaging.

And she trumped by claiming – as true is – that the packaging and its design are different from then, even on the ordinary butter, which is not organic. But despite this argument, which she herself thought was very convincing, Uncle Ola did not give up. Once in a while, he could get really stubborn when it came to it.

So, after a number of long further discussions about it, it had ended up with a compromise: every other day, when it was Aunt Marna who made the morning tea, the French bread was smeared with organic butter, and every other day, when it was Uncle Ola who cooked it, it was with butter that was not organic.

Another important point was imposed on the French bread sandwiches. But here, on the other hand, there was no wavering or disagreement between the spouses. Fortunately, you could say, there was here a point where they were in complete agreement. This is where the tradition lay down. In exactly the same way as it had done at the customs office in its day. At least as far as the broad guidelines were concerned. a piece with cheese, a piece of strawberry jam, and a piece with orange jam.

When it became more concrete, there could well be problems. For example, when it came to cheese. For what kind of cheese would it be? Unfortunately, Aunt Marna had forgotten what type of cheese was used for the customs morning time. Or probably her father had never mentioned it further at home, but simply said a piece of french bread with cheese. So it could be anything, and therefore there had to be free blow for Aunt Marna and Uncle Ola. So it changed a little what kind of cheese it was. Nothing too fancy or special. So it depended on quite a bit of their personal taste, and according to what was on offer in the local supermarket's cheese department.

Strangely enough, they didn't buy the cheese for their morning tea at the local cheese merchant. For one, there was actually still there in the city, admittedly down the other end of the main street. But it was because he was so expensive with his cheese. Much more expensive than Bruges. And when it didn't matter so much, exactly what kind of cheese it was supposed to be. They didn't care much about that.

Different in terms of strawberry jam. For here, Aunt Marna remembered that her father had repeatedly said that it was a very special and fantastically good and tasty strawberry jam, which Miss Petersen herself picked at the customs office herself picked several glasses of each summer of strawberries, which she had been allowed to pick in her neighbour's large garden for a modest fee, either in money or whatever it was. , where there was row after row with strawberry plants of several different varieties.

She obviously made sure every year to pick up so many glasses of the amazing strawberry jam that there were both for herself and her many guests and of course especially to the customs officers at the customs office throughout the winter and spring through until it was summer and strawberry season again. Her father, the father of Aunt Marna, the customs officer, had repeatedly said it was simply the best strawberry jam he had ever tasted. By the way, he always called it jam, not jam.

But what's more, he thought she had to put some special ingredients in, of some kind, to make it taste so amazingly good. Admittedly, she used strawberries of 4-5 different varieties with slightly different flavours in a very specific mixing ratio – she had once told him that, but apparently without mentioning the names of the different strawberry varieties. And he didn't think that in itself was enough to explain the amazing taste.

And then they were on it, because they knew nothing at all about Miss Petersen's special recipe for strawberry jam. They had no idea what had become of her after she had retired decades ago. If she was still alive, she had to be toad-old, at least 90, or perhaps rather around the 100, and probably lived in a nursing home somewhere that they had no idea where they were.

In the end, after a lot of talk back and forth, marna and Ola had agreed that it might be good enough if they bought some really quality strawberry jam (not jam) in the slightly more expensive price range – and of course without added dyes and stuff like that, because they were at least quite sure that miss Petersen used that kind of thing, at least not. It should preferably be something where the label said it was "homemade strawberry jam", or "made according to a traditional recipe" or something like that.

With the orange jam, it was a little easier, it seemed. And yet. Moster Marna meant to remember the name of the special orange jam that had always been used at the customs office during her father's time. It was a buying jam. Of a very specific English brand. But unfortunately it turned out that this special product was no longer being negotiated in this country, even though they were around the many different stores to ask for it.

In the end, however, they managed to get the local cheese merchant to take it home as special imports exclusively for them, although it was admittedly at a hamper price, about 4-5 times as much as a glass of plain good orange jam cost, for example at Irma. But then it had to be that way, they meant. Because it was important that it was as authentic as possible. That's what was at the heart of it all.

And thus, most of it was in place, at least in the big lines. Except the the tea itself, of course. And yet, because a great deal has already been said about this. We must, of course, start with the most important and central thing, which we have therefore done.

But the accident was here, unfortunately, there were two very different perceptions of it in Aunt Marna and Uncle Ola. Fortunately, they had quite learned to live with that gradually.

Although it must be admitted that Uncle Ola was sometimes getting one of Marna's new and particularly spicy or perfumed thes wrong in the throat. And although aunt Marna occasionally (but also only once in a while, it must be said) complained that Uncle Ola perpetually and always, year in and year out, stuck to exactly the same familiar it, so that once in a while (but only once in a while) she called for just a little bit of variation and renewal on his part. Whether this also applied in other areas does not apply to this text; here we deal only with the tea.

A visit to the Christmas market

The park is covered in snow. Like the whole city. It's been snowing again tonight. White Christmas. Maybe. Because there's still a week until Christmas. It's not something I care about very much. Still, I've gone to the big Christmas market in the park. Mostly because I'm bored. Got nothing else to do.

It's Sunday afternoon. It's full of people everywhere. Parents with children who are pestering to get something. The candy stalls are going on. Older people, old men and fat wives. They walk around and look at the different stalls. Maybe they're looking for something for their grandchildren. There are plenty of stalls with all sorts of junk. But it goes like hot bread. At several of the stalls there is a queue to get to. There are also stalls with mulled wine and draught beer and coffee. And with food of different kinds. Burnt almonds and roasted chestnuts. And popcorn.

I'll buy you a bag of popcorn and a coke. I'll move on. There's also a stall with a fortune teller. No, it's not a fortune teller anyway. She sells time travel. That sounds a little exciting. It's available. I'm going to go there. Asking what it costs. A fiftieth, she says. I'm

going to pull out a fiftieth and give her. I
don't usually wear banknotes in my pocket.
Actually, I didn't think I had any at all. But
now all of a sudden there's someone right
here where I need it. She doesn't take mobile
pay or dankort. Cash only. Maybe to create
an atmosphere of the old days.

It's only trips to the past that she sells. Not
for the future. That's why I got interested.
But now I've paid, there's no turning back,
she says. And strangely enough, I just obey
without even protesting or asking why. I
don't usually do that.

She tells me to close my eyes. I close my
eyes. She says a strap I need to repeat. I
repeat it. She says another thong. I repeat it.
She says another thong. I repeat it. She tells
me to open my eyes again. I'm going to open
my eyes again.

People look different than before. At least
their clothes do. The way you've seen it on
old movies. Such from about 100 years ago

maybe. All the things in the park also look old-fashioned. All the stuff at the stalls and the way the stalls are made. It's like I'm dumped in an old movie. Or a TV show set 100 years ago. It's really weird.

Almost everyone in the park wears thick old-fashioned coats, in grey and brownish colours. Everything looks more gray, and more poor. There are not nearly as many colors, either on the clothes or on the stalls. People's hairstyles are also quite different, especially women's. The children's clothes are completely different. The praam wagons look like something from a museum. Everything looks very old-fashioned. Pretty ugly, most of it. Grey, grey, grey. People also talk differently, like that more. And a lot of the adults smoke. Mostly the men. Not so much the women.

The men dominate it all quite a lot. The women and children mostly seem to be just correcting what the man in the family says they should. The children seem improbably stylish and good.

The men are wearing a soft hat and long coats, and the women are wearing ugly and unfixable clothes. Many of them look poor and devastated. Some of them munch hungry on something resembling a piece of dry rye bread. They don't look very happy. And very poor. Some are wearing clothes that are patched.

Somewhere on the edge of the park, behind some trees and shrubs, there are some women who look like whores. In the snow nearby there are some used condoms. It looks disgusting. One of them is about to put his clothes in order. Then she freshens up her lipstick and lights a cigarette. Another of them takes a small bottle of some booze out of his bag and takes a sip of it. Then a man comes to her. They talk a little bit. Then he gives her a couple of old-fashioned notes and they walk around the back of some bushes a little away.

It's starting to snow more heavier. Big snowflakes swirling down. But I think I'm going to have to stay here for a while. Until this time travel is over. I forgot to ask how long it will last, and now I've come out of the stall of time travel. It's actually a little weird if you start thinking about it, like you're trapped in a time warp sometime in the past. Which you haven't even chosen. She didn't even ask me how far I wanted to go back in time and where. She's just pulling lots of it, maybe? Or does she decide for herself where she wants to send people in the past? That's what she just wants to do.

But I guess it's just 2 minutes or half an hour. Or does it? Actually, I don't know! Maybe I should stay here in the past for the rest of the day. Or right up until they close here in the park. Or maybe it goes on for longer still. But where should I go when the

Christmas market closes? The more I think about it, the more sinister it becomes. Or longer still. What if I'm stranded in this time warp and can't get back to my own time again? I don't want to do that!!

Does the time travel end by itself? Or is it the lady who has to do something to end the time journey and bring one back to the present again? Well, what was the present before I got into this time warp. Because now, it's actually the present. Well, right now. I wish I hadn't said yes to this at all.

And what if that lady forgets to bring people back from those time pockets in the past. Or if she forgets exactly how many there are. I'm sure there's more than me. What if, for example, she remembers wrong and thinks she is only 8 people she has sent on a time trip, whereas in reality it is 9. And then there's one of them who gets forgotten inside this time warp and doesn't get picked up again. You're going to stay in this part of the past forever.

There had to be something like an emergency brake you could use if you suddenly wanted to get out of this time travel and back to the present that you came from. It's not very fun to be such a place in the past. Especially if you can't decide for yourself how long it should last and how to get back. But maybe I can find some of the others that are on time travel. They must be wearing modern clothes, just like me.

It is strange, in fact, that none of these people in the park notice me, because I wear clothes other than them. Almost like I can see them, but they can't see me. Like I'm invisible to them or something. That's how it actually works.

But I must be able to spot the others who are on time travel quite easily, because they also stand out with much more smart and modern clothes. But maybe there are only a few in the whole park, and then it might be hard to find them. Because it's not safe. She may find it more fun to send each of them back to a different time in the past. I'd probably think that's more fun if I were her.

But then I also think I would bring them back pretty quickly, maybe after half an hour, and then I would get them to tell you a little about what they had experienced in the time warp I had sent them back to. And I would certainly tell them how long the time travel lasted, even in advance, before they even said yes to it.

But if she can do that with arranging time travel, why doesn't she go on a lot of time travel herself for some really exciting times in the past, instead of just standing there in such a stall and sending others off on time travel. That must be pretty boring. No, of course she doesn't, she probably just wants to make some money from it, although I think she could make a lot more money by selling sweets or cakes or sodas or some other stuff like that.

I know that it's not like the adventurers, with a witch like that, luring children into a time journey, so they're stranded in a time warp that they can get out of themselves, and then she takes them somewhere to a gloomy and creepy house where she keeps them trapped. It's only in those old adventures, and only kids believe in something like that. I've grown from that long ago.

But now I'm going to go around and look at some of the stuff at this Christmas market. Although it is quite different and much more old fashioned. It's not nearly as nice. But there are some things that are still quite fun to look at precisely because they are different. It's kind of like being in a museum with a whole lot of old stuff. Where there are a whole lot of people walking around who are also dressed like in the old days.

Somewhere there's a man playing in a liquor store like I once saw in a real museum. Such a big box where you have to turn around on a crant of hands all the time, and then some music comes out of it that doesn't sound very good. There are some people standing around the man with the lire box listening to the music. I've also stopped to look at it.

Now comes a young man walking with an old wheelbarrow that is made of wood. He's got some very shot pants and a coat with one sleeve on it. On the wheelbarrow there is a small cupboard. There are glass panes in the cabinet doors and three shelves inside the closet, where there are some old books. Not very many. He opens the closet and spreads the books out on the shelves so it looks like a little more. Apparently, they're going to try to sell to people. They look old and worn out. The covers on them are completely different from the way you do it today. They're actually quite ugly. Or it's something that's drawn in such a slightly clumsy way.

There are a few of them who have stood and listened to the man with the lirebox who goes to look at the books and flip a little in them, then there is a woman who buys one of them, but when she has gone for a little piece, she loses the book, which she just holds her hand because someone comes over and asks her something. She hasn't discovered that she's lost it, and just moves on while talking eagerly with the man who came up to her. They might be boyfriends or something, and maybe she's been surprised to suddenly meet him here in the park, so that's mostly what she's thinking about.

So now the book is just lying there in the snow. I run over and pick it up and will run after her to give it to her, but she is already far away and must have turned down another path or about behind something, because now I can't spot her anywhere. So I'm just sticking the book in my pocket. Maybe I'll spot her later somewhere else in the park, I think.

I'll move on. I'm just kind of around a little bit on the must and get and look at some of the different things. It's not that wildly exhilarating, rather a little half-boring. Kind of like a really boring hour at school, just sitting and waiting for the bell to ring out. I just don't know how long it's going to last.

I'm trying to find something that's a little interesting to look at so I don't get bored too much while I'm waiting to get back to the time I'm coming from. My ordinary present. So this isn't a very good advertisement for time travel. If that lady wants to start her business and sell a lot of time travel, I think she should make them a little more exciting than this.

I have now come to one of the big, wide paths in the park. There are a lot of people here, but they look just as poor as the others. There are many of them who go so fast and purposefully as if there is a particular place they are going. I'll follow them to see what it is.

A little further along there is a place with several stalls right next to each other. These are some food stalls. That's where they're headed. At the first of the stalls they serve soup in some small bowls. There's a long queue already. The soup is boiling or kept warm in a huge saucepan that looks almost like an oil barrel. It's almost as big, anyway. Behind the counter there are three rather thick half-old ladies and are busy pouring soup into the small bowls with a large soup spoon. The contents of the spoon fit the hatch with what may be in the bowl.

Then they reach the bowl of the steaming soup to the front of those standing in line and waiting. It doesn't look like they're paying anything for the soup. So apparently it's free. But I think it was something you used sometimes in the old days, things like handing out free food to the poor.

Most people eat the soup in a hurry, as if they are very hungry. Some of them, especially the men, don't even use a spoon to eat it with. Then they wipe their mouths with their sleeves and rush back to the queue for a bowl of soup. It must not be fun to be so poor. They also look pretty sad.

It's still snowing pretty powerfully. Such really big snowflakes that swirl down and lay all over the place. Except if the snowflakes land in the soup. Then they melt right away. But everywhere else, the snowfall keeps growing. Now that I think about it, I think it wasn't until I got out on this time trip to the old days that it started snowing so heavily. Otherwise it would have stopped snowing. Back then when I came into this park for the Christmas market, before I went to that booth with the time travel. I mean that. But it doesn't really matter now.

I've started to get hungry myself, but I don't want to stand up at the back of the long queue for the big soup pot. It's not exactly soup I want the most. But I don't think there's anywhere where you can buy some more modern food.

I'm looking at the other stalls with food. The right next door, sells something that looks like thick slices of rye bread with butter on. Nothing else. No cold cuts. Just a thin layer of butter. No, I don't think it's even butter. Rather, something like that, frying fat or something. The lady sprinkles some coarse salt on from a small tub before handing it to people. But I don't think they're paying anything for it either. So it's probably like a free food distribution for the poor, too. First a bowl of soup, or maybe two, and then a thick slice of rye bread with a little fat on it. That doesn't sound very exciting. Imagine if it was the kind of thing they had to settle for every day. The poor, that is. And I think there were a lot more sfs back then. It's very good that it's just a time trip I'm on. I don't think it's been much fun back then.

And now I'm going back to my own present again soon. What if something happened to her with the time travel so she can't bring people back to the present again?

But there's no point in thinking about it now. I just have to try to have patience and then count on her to have a proper check on it, just concentrate on where I am now. What they call being present in the present. Or now it must be to be present in the da. Is that what it's called? Well, it doesn't matter. But that's where I am now.

I'm going to go a little further, to the next one of the food stalls. But it looks just as boring. But I think it's all for the poor, too.

A modern Day Romeo and Juliet

I'll tell you what. That piece about Romeo and Juliet that you've been about in the studio. You could do that a little differently. Otherwise it will be so trivial if it always just has to stay the same.

What I'm thinking about, it's something like this: Romeo is some kind of zombie, or some kind of robot, or something. Or no, it was something else I came up with. If we're going to update it a little bit to the present and stuff like that. So both Romeo and Juliet are participants in such a reality show on TV. And then Romeo is burned hot on Juliet, but TVProducer Don't want the two to get together. For he has appointed another, which Julie must form a couple Med because he thinks they fit better together, and that it fits better with the concept if it's Julie and him the other. And then he puts all sorts of obstacles in the way of Romeo and Juliet. Or maybe it's a female producer, and that's because she sélv Has gotten hot on Romeo and wants him himself, not on TV, but outside in the real world, because she can see that he is really in love with Juliet and doesn't just want a quick with her. And then it's her. The TV producerThat makes a lot of trouble for Romeo and Juliet so they don't get each other, and that's why she's creating all those difficulties that make it hard for them. Have Julie. And the TV procedure runs both itself and the whole situation further and further out. All the way into the hemp actually. But the more she tries to get in his pants, the more he focuses on Julie and only on Julie. Eventually, it becomes a pure power struggle between the TV producer and Romeo. The TV producer can't just send Julie off the show, because she's the star of the show and without her the viewership would drop dramatically. Then the TV producer tries to get one of the other men in the programme to flierte with Julie. Of course, she doesn't fall for that. Then she'll try the next one. And the next one. And the next one. Until she's been all the male contestants through. Some of them she has to even sleep with to persuade them to do it because they themselves are burned heat on one of the other girls and don't turn on so much on Julie's Type. By mistake, the TV producer's hefty sex with the other men is filmed and joins the broadcast. Or maybe it's because one of the technicians or photographers is mad at the TV producer because she's rejected his advances. So now he wants to take revenge on her by making sure that the sex scenes with her are included in the broadcasts. The tv station boss is considering firing the TV producer because it is a clear violation of the rules of the broadcast. But the hefty sex scenes with the TV producer make viewership rise enormously, so he doesn't fire her after all. He demands more sex scenes between the TV producer and the male contestants, but now they've had enough of her, so to get the viewer numbers back up he'll have to sleep with her himself and make sure it's filmed and joins in Broadcast. But one of the female contestants has gone mad at the TV producer for luring him, on whom she was most burned, to sleep with her, that is, with the TV producer, and she is so angry about that, so she swaps the TV boss's Viagrapills with some lime pellets, and then he can't get it up, as it comes down to the play and the film crew is already filming it live. Viewers are, of course, furious about this, and

viewership plummets. Now the TV boss has
to come up with something in a hurry if he
doesn't want to lose his job. Fortunately,
though, there is Romeo and Juliet, who have
caused so much trouble throughout the
broadcasts, but are nonetheless the most
popular with viewers. But what he's
proposing now, they won't be part of either.
So he gets one of the most underpaid by the
technicians to put a heavy sleeping remedy
in the drinks to be served to Romeo and
Juliet at a particularly wild party. But he's
just an unemployed person who's been sent
to job training at the tv station, and unlike
most people, he doesn't really bother with
that TV thing because he'd rather just sit at
home and smoke weed all the time. And that
very day he really went to it with the gala
before he was supposed to show up for work.
So by mistake, he will give Romeo's drink to
the TV producer and Juliet's drink to an old
cleaning wife from Lithuania who has come
to clean a completely different studio on the

tv station, but finds it difficult to find her way around the place because she has only just started work a fortnight ago and does not speak Danish and the signage is under all the criticism. So instead of Romeo and Juliet, it's going to be the tv procedure and the Lithuanian cleaning wife that falls into the each other's arms as distraught lovers who cannot have each other. Meanwhile, Romeo and Juliet, who for once are not being supervised by the TV producer, go out to one of the toilets in the side wing and get their first real bang on the tv station's territory. Without thinking that there are security cameras in all the toilets, so their lovemaking meeting is still filmed and broadcast, even if it is in incredibly poor image quality. But tv viewers love the clip and viewership rises again. But then...

...hello, are you even listening? It's Mom trying to tell you something. Are you there...

...the sound from the TV is so loud I can't hear what you're saying? If you say something. I think it was a great idea for one of your favorite tv shows. But it's the usual thing you don't want to hear about mom's advice, right?

Almost the usual story

Here she was, all alone, and didn't even really know where to go. But she hadn't heeded his advice. She had found out early on that her mother was in the same situation as herself. So she couldn't help her either.

She had had a couple of affairs with other guys. But each time it had been short-lived and she hadn't felt anything special about it.

It was with sadness that she thought of him. For three long years she had seen nothing of him and heard nothing from him. She was so looking forward to meeting him again.

She looked around and watched the surroundings intensely. It was like it was the first time she saw them right. She had to walk alone with all her anxiety and her problems and try to bite it all.

Then she started to go on the must and get. She had never been in love like that before. He was so manly. The mother was so scared, she didn't dare say anything to him. Now she regretted it, but now it was too late.

Maybe, after all, there was a way out if she just kept going. And it was all his fault. Now it was finally going to happen with their marriage.

And then all of a sudden it was over all together, as suddenly as it had begun.

What was she doing here, too? She had always been afraid of him. Ever since then, when he had first over-fussed her. I wish there would soon be a turnaround for the better, she thought. She had longed so unspeakably. She had fallen for him at first sight, and she still found his charm equally irresistible. Despite everything that had happened.

Now it was all going to be all right, she thought.

But then dark clouds had suddenly pulled over the horizon, and the storm had rapidly moved closer. And now it was all over. In the early days, she had not been able to believe that it was true, but slowly she had woken up to reality and had had to face the facts.

It had simply been the love of her life. Maybe you only really loved once in a lifetime, as some people said, she thought bitterly. She envied the thick mantle that lay at home in the hook by the oven and slept sweetly.

Her mother was not able to help her, although she may have wanted to. But then she came to terms with the deal. She had to make sure to keep her share of it. Even though he had always advised her from it, that is, the deal, the old agreement. But she didn't care about that now.

She took a roof in herself and realized she had to move on. There was no point in continuing to dwell on the memories. She imagined what the beautiful ceremony would be like, and was almost at the thought. Maybe it could still be done.

Was love like that? She thought. But from the familiar edge there was probably no help to get. She had to take care of it herself.

For the time being, she had waited in vain. When she reached the yard, she slowed down. She could take it a little more easy now. It was nice not to have to stress so much. They had only known each other for a week when they started getting together. And she knew that sometimes he stood by his word, and she had run a test on him. His truthfulness was as high as 54, more than most others she had known.

He had made a promise to her the last time they were together. Implied, of course. Sometimes she even blushed when she came to think of it, but there was no time for that now.

She had to go home and feed the cat. She didn't bother to wait for him anymore in the cold and creepy backyard. She must have misunderstood the message he had given her. Now she had to go home and make dinner and have a romantic movie on TV. And feed the cat. That was almost the most important thing.

She saw him for a long time. But now she saw him for herself when she began the long home trip along the winding little streets, where it could be difficult to find your way if you were not well known. And she wasn't. Not in this part of town. It had been so many years since she was last here. But now

she saw him clearly for herself, the big fat
vom, the week-old stubble, all the double
chins, and the little prickly pig eyes that had
so often looked at her with a mocking
expression. She had hated school. She still
did it, so many years later.

Despite the sunshine gently peeing behind an
almost white cloud, she couldn't be happy.
How could she do that when it was as it was?
When the thought of him kept nagging? She
wishes she hadn't gone there. Had she
misunderstood him?

She continued along the increasingly sun-
drenched street. In between, she looked up at
the tall red houses. She had already come
well away from the backyard. She was
happy about that. She walked with healthy
steps and even slowed down. She had to go
home and feed the cat. That's what she had
to do.